ERIC
THE LIONTAMER

Written by
Rachel Elliot

Illustrated by
Uwe Mayer

little bee

Eric and Snail are practising.

Eric is going to be a lion tamer.

Snail is going to be an acrobat.

"Time to go," says Eric.

"You'd better be quick,
before it starts!" calls Eric.
"Before what starts?" asks Mum.

But Eric is in too much of a hurry.

There is a small centipede sitting on the pavement.

"Fancy being a stunt centipede?" asks Eric.

The centipede seems quite keen.

He already knows a few tricks.

(Eric picks him up and puts him in his pocket.)

Eric meets Mrs Hodges.
"Hurry up, or you'll be late!" says Eric.
"Late for what?" asks Mrs Hodges.
But Eric spots a little mouse sitting
on the wall.

"Would you like to be a tightrope walker?" asks Eric.

"You could have a spangly costume."

The mouse seems to like the idea.

(Eric puts the mouse on his shoulder.)

The postman rides past.

"Better deliver your letters fast!" calls Eric.

"You don't want to miss it!"

"Miss what?" asks the postman.

But Eric sees three dogs,
mooching by the dustbins.

"Want to be clowns?" asks Eric.
The dogs fall over themselves in excitement!

"Then follow me," says Eric.

Eric's school looks different.

There is candy floss for sale in the classroom.

There is a fortune teller in the staff room.

There is a crowd of people in the playground.

Everyone cheers when they see Eric.
"It's starting! It's starting!"
they shout.

It's all up to Eric!

He scratches his head and thinks fast.

"Quick, do something!"

he whispers to the three dogs.

No sooner said than done!
The dogs start clowning around.
They trip over each other!
They throw custard pies!

"We love it!
What's next?" cheers the crowd.

The mouse jumps onto the tightrope.

She balances!

She backflips!

She holds on with her tail and swings!

"Wow! What's next?" the crowd whoops.

The centipede
takes centre stage.

He bungee
jumps
without
a crash
helmet!

He does the splits!
The crowd goes wild!
"What's next?" they shout.

Snail gulps.
Eric launches
him up, **up**, **UP**
in the air!
He flies!
He does fifty
roly-polies!

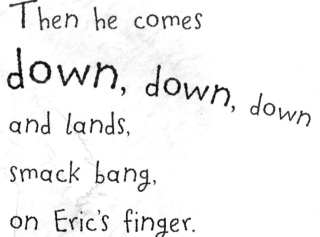

Then he comes
down, **down**, down
and lands,
smack bang,
on Eric's finger.

What a performance!
"Brilliant! What's next?" cheers the crowd.

There is a terrible roar!

Everyone screams!

The centipede clutches Snail!

The mouse clutches her whiskers!

The dogs hide behind Eric!

It's a huge... hairy... hulking...

Eric looks the lion straight in the eye.
"You ought to be ashamed of yourself,
scaring people like that!" says Eric.
The lion looks quite embarrassed.
It stops roaring.

"Now sit there quietly and behave yourself!"
says Eric, crossly. "And if you're good,
I might just find a job for you."

"Roll up, roll up!" calls Eric. "Buy your tickets from the lion at the door."

Quick before it starts!

For
Ali and Sarah,
with love
R.E

For
Zöe and Squirrel,
U.M.

First published in 2004 by Meadowside Children's Books,
185 Fleet Street, London, EC4A 2HS

This edition published in 2008 by Little Bee
an imprint of Meadowside Children's Books

Text © Rachel Elliot Illustration © Uwe Mayer 2004
The rights of Rachel Elliot to be identified as the author and Uwe Mayer
to be identified as the illustrator of this work have been asserted by them in
accordance with the Copyright, Designs and Patents Act, 1988

A CIP catalogue record for this book is available from the British Library
Printed in Malaysia

10 9 8 7 6 5 4 3 2